MW00973231

What Is There To Do In The Country?

Mary Lane Reed   *Ben Douglas*

By Ben Douglas
Illustrated by Mary Lane Reed

Sontag Press

Copyright © 1995 by Ben Douglas
Published by Sontag Press in 1995
P.O. Box 1487, Madison, MS 39130
800/497-3172
Exclusive Distribution by Southern Publishers Group
800/628-0903

Illustrations by Mary Lane Reed
Book Design by Lori Leath-Smith

Library of Congress Cataloging-in-Publication Data
Douglas, Ben, 1935—
What Is There To Do In The Country/by Ben Douglas

ISBN 1-885483-00-7

Printed in the United States of America

To
The residents of Sontag,
past and present
—B.D.

To
Mark, Danny, Mary Moore
and David
—M.R.

John and Lucas jumped out of bed.
The rooster was crowing. There were animals to be fed.

They live on a farm deep in the woods.

They have as much fun as anyone could.

John and Lucas had waited for this day.
Cousin Rupert from the city was coming to stay.

Rupert came to stay a whole week.
His mama said, "Mind your manners,
and always play sweet."

"Golly, this place is boring. It's dullsville," said Rupert
to Lucas and John.
"What could you ever do here to have any fun?"

The next morning, they had hot biscuits for breakfast
with homemade molasses.
They had ham and eggs and milk from bright jelly glasses.

They fed the chickens and the cows,
then they gathered some eggs.

They watched the new calf walk about
on his wobbly legs.

They chopped some wood and did they hustle!
They worked up appetites and built up muscles.

They watched the dog chase rabbits,
and they gathered fresh corn.
They carried it to the house in sacks that were torn.

They drew water from the well. They hauled in the hay.
They put milk in a churn, and made butter the next day.

Rupert learned to plow a straight furrow—he walked back and forth.
After the plowing was all done, they rode home on the horse.

They rested in the shade and told tall tales.

They gathered red tomatoes in large, deep pails.

They swam in the creek, and climbed up a tree.
They ate fresh vegetables, and drank lots of tea.

They rode in a block-wheeled wagon, and built a toy train,
And one day they played in the warm, summer rain.

They played on a tire swing beneath the big oak tree.

They played a game of marbles while kneeling on one knee.

Rupert tried as best he could to milk old bossy the cow.
By the end of the week, he was beginning to learn how.

On Friday they got 10 cents each, and they ran out the door,
down to the crossroads to the little country store.

In the store there were drinks for five cents
and enough goodies to please.
And there was a great big hoop of some very good cheese.

There was no movie theatre to which they could go,
so they hung up a sheet and put on a shadow show.

Each night Rupert was tired and into the bed he did creep.
"Poor Rupert," said Lucas, "he was so bored he fell asleep."

But the next day they were at it again—
working and playing and exploring places
that Rupert had never been.

When Rupert's mama came to get him,
he was still having fun.

"Don't take me home, yet," he said.
"There are things to do here that I have never done."